Blessed II

A LIFE TRANSFORMED

By Harry L. Williams II

 ISBN: 9798323829514

Preface

Welcome to Blessed II, the latest captivating novel written by Bishop Harry L. Williams II. Whether you've read the prequel "Blessed" or not, this book promises to push the boundaries of faith, perseverance, and redemption to new heights.

As a testament to the transformative power of God's love, Blessed II continues the journey of our hero Wood, echoing the author's own remarkable story. In this gripping narrative, we find Wood devoted to serving the Lord, nurturing young minds, and confronting the forces of darkness. Through trials and triumphs, Bishop Harry L. Williams II masterfully weaves a tale of hope, inspiration, and unwavering commitment to one's purpose. Along the way we gain deeper insight into the lives of Ray, Vanessa, and Pastor Williams and how their decisions impact their blessings. As the story unfolds, the author masterfully explores the complexities of their relationships revealing the power of revival, belief, and forgiveness.

As you delve into these pages, prepare to be immersed in a world of drama, action, and salvation where the struggle is real but God's presence is palpable.

This book is more than a sequel – it's a testament to the human spirit's capacity for growth, restoration, and love. Join Bishop Harry L. Williams II as he skillfully guides us through the triumphs and tribulations of Wood's unforgettable journey as we are reminded that with faith, anything is possible.

Table of Contents

CHAPTER ONE

The Game

The brakes on Wood's car screeched as he slowed down to find the right house. All the houses in this neighborhood looked the same: freshly mowed lawns, warm, inviting front porches, and nothing out of place. The only difference that stood out at this particular house was a few cars parked out front, while the rest of the driveways in the neighborhood were empty.

I told myself that this part of my life was over; I learned to conquer my ego and knew that money wasn't the answer to everything. Yet, I was still trying to make things work on my own.

Ray hopped out of the car, put his cigarette out on the curb, and slammed the door.

Wood grabbed his black bag and made his exit, shaking his head as he noticed the neighbor's eyes peeking through the slits of their blinds.

"It's going to be a good day, homie. Let's make this quick. I've got some bait on the line." That's the thing about Ray – he's trustworthy and a good friend, but sometimes naïve to the game. He never quite understands how quickly situations can turn bad. On the other hand, that's what I love about this dude – nothing seems to bother him.

The two approached the house, and Wood knocked on the door three times. Immediately after, a low and gruff bark echoed from inside and after waiting a minute for someone to come to the door, Ray grew fidgety. Seeing Ray's restlessness, Wood knocked again.

"Yeah?" a voice replied, followed by the door opening. The homeowner, a large man with no neck, stood in front of them.

His muscular build and imposing presence filled the doorway with his large mustache bristling as he stared at Wood. It was clear that Wood was an unwelcome disturbance, an inconvenience.

Undeterred, Wood offered the muscled man a disarming smirk, hoping to lighten the mood. He knew this game; his logistical mindset and people skills made him successful, but also got him into trouble in the past. Enforcing rules and not letting matters go unhandled led to violent situations. In the streets, reputation was everything; weakness was not an option.

Wood, whose smirk grew more sinister, shifted his jacket to reveal what he had for the homeowner, just in case he had any intentions besides handling business.

The homeowner's stare lingered on Ray, who stood oblivious with his usual goofy grin. "He's with me. He's cool," Wood reassured the homeowner.

The homeowner's hand hovered near his waist gun with his eyes fixed on Ray, who was fiddling with his phone. A stern look from Wood prompted Ray to pocket his phone.

"Hey, I said don't worry about him. We doing this or not?"

The homeowner stepped aside, finally allowing Wood and Ray to enter. Ray's goofy grin disappeared as he surveyed the interior of the house. Despite its picture-perfect exterior, the inside told a different story. The beautiful house itself was familiar to Ray. As a broker, he'd seen plenty of homes like this before; this client's home was another matter. Thick smoke hung in the air, and an inescapable tension permeated every room they passed through, with each one monitored by surveillance cameras.

Ray knew from experience to stay vigilant and keep his head on a swivel. The last thing he wanted was to get caught slipping again.

As they walked through the house, the homeowner swung doors open to reveal people in various states. Through the crack in one door, Ray saw a couple of guys zoned out on video games, like they were in a trance.

Voices echoed from down the hall, a group of men either arguing or laughing - it was hard to tell. Ray and Wood followed a woman in and out of consciousness up the stairs and into a room. Once upstairs, Wood was taken into a room without Ray who was left alone waiting anxiously.

"What's up with the babysitters, Wood? Normally, I see you alone. Different circumstances now, I guess. We good, right?" After he finished the transaction, Wood exited the room, Ray trailed behind, exhaling a quiet sigh of relief.

They walked past the gamers at the entrance of the living room and into a massive kitchen with gleaming white marble countertops.

As they walked down a hallway with towering walls, Ray's phone rang, and Wood nodded for him to answer. Ray stepped outside to take the call, feeling safer in the fresh air. Just as they reached the front door, an elderly man called out,

"Wood! Hey, man! I thought that was you!"

Wood recognized the man's voice immediately - it was Antonio, an old friend from the block.

Wood remembered Antonio was well respected, not only for his success but also for his calm and collected demeanor in every situation.

"Antonio, it's been a minute!" Wood exclaimed, as the two men shook hands in a warm greeting. "Never thought I'd see you here," Antonio said with a chuckle.

Wood placed a hand on Antonio's shoulder, and guiding him out the front door, Ray continued ahead, still preoccupied on his phone call.

Wood saw this as the perfect opportunity to ask Antonio something he had been working up the courage to ask for a while.

"I'm trying to get out the game, man. I want to start over. I'm just about ready to buy that pool hall we use to talk about."

Wood knew that buying the pool hall would be a fresh start, but he wasn't certain if Antonio was willing to sell it, let alone to him.

Asking about it was a gamble, and Antonio's response would reveal if his dream was possible. Antonio's eyes moved from Wood to the house they just left, and a thoughtful look crossed his face.

Antonio looked at Wood, then looked back at the house they just left with a serious expression on his face. "Remember what I said way back when? You can't get your money out of the game if you're still in the game."

Wood shifted his weight from side to side, unsurprised by Antonio's blunt words. This dude was a straight shooter, and if anyone was going to give it to him raw, it was Antonio. Wood was embarrassed knowing he had been seen at that house in the middle of the day by one of the only people whose opinion mattered.

Antonio pointed at Wood, his voice stern. "When you're serious, we'll revisit the conversation, young blood."

Wood knew Antonio was right – he always was. Still, Wood couldn't shake off that feeling of defeat.

He knew he needed to be done with all of this, but it was never that simple. As he walked back to his car, he wondered what he could do to prove his sincerity to Antonio and show him he was serious about starting over and changing his life.

With the last bit of courage he had, Wood popped the trunk, revealing a surprise that might just convince Antonio that he was done playing around.

CHAPTER TWO

The Investment

"Wait, Antonio." The old man cautiously approached Wood's car, unsure what to expect.

"I got something for you.

"Wood held out a stack of cash, trying to steady his hand as he handed it over to Antonio. This was his last chance to prove the sincerity of his offer.

"That's 50 grand. I'll come pick up the keys to the pool hall when I'm out of the game for good. Look, the money is yours - do what you want with it. If I come back, you know I'm serious. If not, that's a large amount to give away as a lesson." Wood continued, "I want you to know how serious I am. I'll take that risk."

Antonio accepted the money, and Wood got back in his car leaving while Antonio stood there staring at the amount of money in his hand.

Ray was still on the phone when Wood got back in the car but quickly hung up the phone and turned to Wood.

"What was that about?" Ray was annoyed as he looked back at Antonio, who watched the two of them drive away. Between the uneasy feeling he had inside the house and seeing his friend hand over what he could only guess was thousands of dollars; Ray knew something big was going down.

"Let's just say I made a little investment in my future," Wood said with a hint of a smile on his face. "I haven't felt this good about spending this much bread in a long time."

Wood's mind wandered as he drove down the street, imagining a life free from the game.

However, his daydream was abruptly interrupted by the persistent ring of Ray's phone.

"Who the heck keeps calling you? Your phone has been blowing up all day," Wood asked, with a hint of suspicion creeping into his voice.

Ray laughed nervously and quickly silenced the phone call, careful not to let Wood see who was on the caller ID. Wood continued to stare, expecting an answer, but Ray looked out the window, fumbling to silence his phone as it began ringing again.

Wood shook his head with a disappointed look on his face. He recognized Ray's potential, but it seemed like his friend was still trapped in a vicious cycle.

"Alright, bruh, do you, and by the way, when are you coming to Bible study like you promised?", Wood asked with concern in his voice. The two had been through a lot together over the years, including getting shot.

Wood wanted Ray to turn his life around too, but his friend was falling deeper and deeper into the game.

Lying in the hospital bed, Wood had promised to change his life and devote himself to God if he ever made it out. Ray, on the other hand, was hesitant, always avoiding the subject of Bible study.

Ray's anxiety spiked when he looked out the window and noticed the traffic coming to a standstill.

Ray dreaded being trapped in a car with Wood on one of his "bible study rants." The tension from Wood's stare made him more agitated.

"Listen, I'm not where you are. I hope to get there one day. Right now, I'm just grateful to be alive - I know it was God, no question. But stop asking me when I'll come to Bible study! I'm going to attend. I'll get there when it's time. I promise. What do I look like sitting up in church when I'm out here in these streets?

What if people from the church saw me? I ain't no hypocrite, man. Do what works for you and let me do the same. I promised God that no matter what, I wouldn't kill anyone, and that's all I can commit to right now. There's too much money out here, and I'm trying to get to it. I have goals, too, you know."

Ray knew how important it was to Wood for them to walk together, to turn their lives around, but Ray wasn't ready yet. Knowing that Wood blamed himself, Ray toned it down. "Man, I don't care what anybody says. I ain't going to hell. I'm not going out like that. I got saved for real, man." With an uneasy expression, he repeated himself. "I ain't going to hell. Can we just thank God for the little things? Let's celebrate that. We living. A lot of folks can't say that."

Wood looked at his friend with both sympathy and confusion. He could tell Ray wasn't telling him something.

All he could do was hope that whatever his friend was struggling with would eventually come to the light.

The vehicle came to a stop as the two pulled up in front of Ray's house. Ray knew his friend was upset with him and offered a truce. "Hey, man, let me know how it goes, alright?"

Wood nodded his head and waited for his friend to enter his home before pulling off.

CHAPTER THREE

Messing With Fire

Like every other new convert, Wood finally realized that the street life wasn't for him or anyone else. He also understood that most street cats didn't get to choose the life they lived - they were just trying to survive.

As wood was crossing the street on the way to church, a teenager from the block spotted him and flagged him down.

"Wood, let a brother get a few dollars so I can get something from the store. You know how it is," the teen begged.

"No doubt," Wood agreed, handing him fifty bucks. "How's everything at home?"

"Trying to keep from coming out here, but it's hard," the teen replied.

Wood then pulled up his shirt, revealing his healed wounds. "I almost died twice out here. You better go to school and focus on your education and that dream of yours." Looking around, Wood continued, "There's nothing out here, man, but heartache. Keep it moving in the other direction if you can."

"Thanks, Wood. I got you when I come up." The teen ran off, leaving Wood to continue his journey.

The temptations attached to this new life seemed more overwhelming than those he faced when he was still in the streets. Determined to keep his promise to God, Wood started attending a singles Bible study group led by a fellow church member, Vanessa. He was captivated by her enticing dark skin and her love for the Lord. Her enthusiastic smile was as bright as day.

Wood walked into the Bible study group session and spotted her immediately. She wore a slightly tight red dress, her legs crossed, and Wood almost couldn't contain his smile when she looked in his direction.

How am I supposed to take my eyes off this beauty? He mentally fantasized.

Vanessa's lesson for the night focused on the story of David. Before the discussion ended, she asked one last question. "Wood, what do you think about your man, David?"

"David?" Wood asked, slightly puzzled.

"I think he was messing with fire," one of the other guys from the group interjected. "That guy had third-degree burns!" Everyone burst out laughing.

After Bible study ended, Wood was about to pull out of the parking lot when he spotted Vanessa.

He quickly hopped out of his car and rushed over to where she was, thinking of ways to start a conversation with her. "I'm sorry, I was a bit distracted tonight, I had a couple of things on my mind," he explained, as he reached to open her car door.

"I understand Wood, it happens to the best of us" she replied.

"You did a great job leading the discussion tonight," Wood said, as he placed her bag inside the vehicle. He wanted to say more but felt he was already doing too much.

"Uhm, well. . . good night, Vanessa. See you around," Wood awkwardly turned and walked toward his car, leaving Vanessa puzzled. She couldn't help but gaze at him as he walked away. "What was that all about?" she muttered to herself, as she hopped into her car. At the sound of her car's ignition, she remembered that she had changed the singles meeting schedule and announced it to the class before Wood's arrival.

Being hopeful that Wood would take this opportunity to recover from the earlier awkwardness, she smiled to herself. Plus, she felt he needed to interact with other congregation members more.

She quickly drove over to his car before he pulled off, rolling down her window.

"Wood, I forgot to mention that we're meeting again in a few days. It would be good if you came."

As Wood drove home, he flipped through a few stations. Once home, he realized that he didn't get a date or time from Vanessa.

He decided to give her a call. After a couple of rings, she finally answered.

"This is V." "V?! I got you. Hey, lady, didn't mean to bother you, I got your number from the church directory. I hope that's ok. I realized that we never talked about a time or date."

"Oh yeah, sorry about that. You weren't in class when I mentioned we changed the singles meeting to Wednesdays now. I'm actually glad you called. It would have been a shame if you got there and we weren't there. Besides, that's why my number is in there. Just don't be calling a sister at 2 or 3 in the morning" she teased.

"I wouldn't do you like that... unless it's an emergency. You'd be there, right?" Wood asked.

Vanessa laughed as she replied, "I definitely will, I'm looking forward to it."

The following days felt like years to Wood; he couldn't take his mind off Vanessa's smile and couldn't wait to see it again.

Vanessa had to leave work early because she wanted to get a little rest before Bible study class. Her home was quiet, and she found peace in the solitude of her sanctuary.

As she began to unwind with her daily routine, she decided to break the silence.

"Alexa, play salsa!" she shouted.

"Playing Sada," the electronic voice replied.
Why does this thing test me? "Play SAL-SA!" she shouted with greater emphasis. Salsa music began to play, and she began to unwind, letting her mind venture to past times.

Flashbacks of her old life, which she was so glad to be out of, began to take shape as old images from the past popped up. Just as her mind started to wander into the current situation she was in, she unconsciously fell asleep. In an instant, her ringtone blared from the speakers. She snapped out of her trance in disgust. *God, why can't I get rid of these thoughts, and why are they in my dreams?*

CHAPTER FOUR

Opening Doors And Resisting Temptation

Sliding the chair across the floor, Wood looked to see if anyone noticed his late entrance to the singles meeting. Vanessa noticed and turned toward him.

"Welcome!" She greeted.

There was no response from Wood. It was clear that he didn't hear her as he continued to settle into his seat. Phone in hand, he asked what he missed. They were just moving past the greetings. As she introduced the new visitors, Wood continued to watch and question why God challenged him so soon. His only reason for attending the class in the first place was to build a better relationship with God. Trying to maintain his focus, Wood walked over to the water fountain.

After regaining his composure, he sat back down. He couldn't help but notice how Vanessa talked with her hands. She handled being the center of attention with ease. *I got this, and eventually, I'll have this saved life thing on lock just like her,* Wood thought to himself. Wood saw something in Vanessa. He felt there was more to her story. She spoke with so much wisdom that only an experienced life could have given her. He made a mental note to mention her in his meeting with Pastor Williams on Friday.

Wood glanced through the crowd and recognized his old friend, Rose, walking toward him. She smiled and waved. Rose was with her older brother, whom Wood had yet to meet. After being introduced, the three of them began chatting, and before he knew what was happening, Rose's brother offered Wood a job as a security guard where he worked.

Even though he knew the job would pay far less than what he was used to, he was desperate to make an honest living.

He had to start somewhere, and this job was just the start he needed. Wood agreed to do the job, and the two shook hands. As he turned to get in his car, he gave Rose a big hug and his thanks as they said their goodbyes.

Feeling like freedom was finally within his reach, Wood danced and sang along to the music blasting from his car speakers as he drove home. The streets seemed brighter and more peaceful than usual, which was rare for the time of day it was. The peaceful drive was quickly rattled as the hood of Wood's car suddenly popped open, blocking his view of the street. "What the?!"

Wood began to panic as he tried to pull over. Instead, he ended up driving on the sidewalk and crashing head-on into a traffic pole.

Even though he wasn't driving fast, the airbag shot out and slammed against his head.

Feeling a little dizzy, Wood stepped out of his car and looked around to see if he had hit anyone. Luckily, he was all alone.

Usually, the street would be packed with a mix of people returning from the office, students walking home from school, or general crowds standing around, but somehow it was completely empty. *He began to thank God because Wood knew it could have been so much worse.*

A familiar black and silver SUV Range Rover stopped next to where his car sat smashed against a pole. One tinted window slowly rolled down, revealing the whip's familiar owner.

"Need a ride?"

Wood knew of the guy, Brick. He was a young street hustler. He wasn't exactly the person Wood wanted to see, but he was in no place to turn down a ride since he still was about four miles from his house.

Wood nodded and got into the Range Rover. He gasped when he saw how clean Brick's ride was, not to mention the amenities. It had interior neon lights, and a gigantic GPS displayed on the glass of the driver's windshield.

"Man, Brick, your ride is nicer than my house."

Brick laughed and nodded. "Probably cost more too," he said, half-joking, but it was the truth. Wood sat in the passenger seat, trying not to say much, mostly because he didn't want to go down that drug talk road, but he couldn't help himself.

"Man, I didn't know you were out here making moves like this. Things must be going well to afford a ride like this?"

Turning the steering wheel, Brick met Wood's puzzled gaze and shrugged. He knew Wood's reputation; everyone did.

Brick said, "You know how it is out here. You work, you eat. If you really work, this stuff comes with it. I hear you're semi-retired, Wood... whatever that means."

"I know you're out here hustling, but you could retire as well..." Wood replied.

"That's wishful thinking," Brick chuckled.

After a minute of silence, Wood started again, "I can't believe I crashed my car. I don't need this right now. Today is certainly a money day for me." Speaking of the money he had just invested in the pool hall earlier, he continued, "It's a great thing I got tough skin. I don't even know how that happened."

"If it's not one thing, it's another," Brick muttered. "How much you think you'll need to fix it? I'll give it to you, and you can pay me back whenever."

Wood's eyes opened wide. He was amazed by the generosity of this man he hardly knew, but he knew better than to get involved with someone like Brick.

Especially now when his goal was to exit the game. He knew the devil was trying to set him up. The temptation was real, and he knew that this would be the beginning of nothing if he accepted the money. He could get caught up very easily. The risk wasn't worth it, no matter what Brick had to offer. "Nah, man, don't worry about it. I'm good. I appreciate the offer, though." Wood threw up his hands as he shut the door on the SUV. As he walked up his driveway, he suddenly stopped and turned around. His heart was racing, thinking about how much Brick's offer would help him. Wood wanted to run back and tell Brick he had made a mistake, and he would accept the money, but it was too late. He had already driven off.

CHAPTER FIVE

The Last Time

Pastor Williams greeted Wood with a warm handshake. He was a kind-hearted man with a powerful presence, who easily brought out the best in everyone he met, without discrimination. Wood had witnessed him preaching to homeless men and women on the corners many times. Opening up to Pastor Williams was easy. Wood confessed to being worried about how things were going in his life.

"Sometimes we have faith in God and worry, son; that's just the way it is. The Bible tells us not to be anxious about anything. Romans 14:23 says, "everything that does not come from faith is sin." All of us have to do better if we say we trust Him.

Wood agreed with the Pastor and was consumed with remorse that he was trusting his abilities more than God. He knew that was the right thing to do.

It didn't make it any better that Vanessa had just led a session about the exact same thing.

Wood felt ashamed, so he quickly changed the subject. He began speaking about the job he had recently accepted from Rose's brother. He and Rose had begun to get close, as her brother started attending the single's classes. The subject of the singles class made Wood think of Vanessa.

Pastor Williams immediately noticed the spark in Wood's eyes as he talked. Wood noticed the Pastor's smile. He felt the Pastor was starting to think something about his and Vanessa's relationship, so he immediately stopped what he was saying and shook his head. Wood assured Pastor Williams that she was just a friend, and his focus was on building a better relationship with God.

He just felt it was necessary to be honest with Pastor. Wood smiled at the thought of Vanessa and admitted that she was extremely attractive, smart, and very much saved. Wood admitted with a smile, "Pastor, I can't front.

I wouldn't enjoy the class as much if it wasn't for her."

He also mentioned that Vanessa was leaving town next week and things would not be the same without her. Vanessa often shared stories from her past with the class, and he felt good knowing that he wasn't the only one working towards change. It seemed like they both took steps forward only for something to happen that would tempt them both to stumble back to their old way of doing things.

Wood explained how she grabbed his attention. Her stories always seemed to resonate with him. Some of the things she said made it seem like she was walking in his shoes.

Wood was tempted to do another deal or two after his freak car accident. For Vanessa, the temptation was caused by an eviction notice on her door.

Vanessa came home after a long day at work. She had recently taken a job at a small diner in town.

The customers could be demanding at times, but Vanessa liked it better than her last job. She remained busy, as her schedule was always full as a part-time law student and teacher. All she wanted to do was take a long shower and go to bed. Instead, Vanessa had to face reality as she looked at the giant red piece of paper laughing at her when she went to unlock the door to her apartment. Vanessa hoped nobody saw her struggling to rip the tape off and remove it from the door.

The truth was, she was good at hiding how much she struggled. Nobody knew of the days she stayed hidden in her apartment without getting dressed or eating anything.

Some days it would take all of her energy and strength just to get out of bed. Nobody knew about how helpless she often felt.

Her thoughts often wandered to her life as a stripper. The money situations she was currently facing often made her think about becoming a dancer again.

The eviction notice on the door and harsh realities that came with it knocked her down in a different way. She felt like she was back at square one, and the thought of starting over was overwhelming.

Vanessa took a deep breath and tried to push the thoughts away, but they lingered, taunting her like a constant reminder of her struggles.

As much as Vanessa wanted to hide from the world, she knew something needed to be done. If she got evicted from her apartment, she would have to move back in with her parents.

Her parents were so proud of all the work she was doing, and she didn't want to let them down. Vanessa didn't trust anyone else to ask for a place to stay. The only family she had in town was her sister, who was also struggling with finances and other vices, and Vanessa didn't want to add to her burdens.

Walking through her house, it felt like she was in a haze as she tried to think of her next move.

Vanessa went to her nightstand and picked up her Bible. She sat down on her bed and turned the pages until she found what she was looking for. She quietly began to read aloud while fighting back tears, Matthew 11:28-30: *"Come to me, all you who are weary and burdened, and I will give you rest. Take my yoke upon you and learn from me, for I am gentle and humble in heart, and you will find rest for your souls. For my yoke is easy and my burden is light."*

Feeling a bit calmer and like she could see clearly for the first time all day; Vanessa closed her eyes and began to doze off with her Bible in her hand. "Quack! Quack! Quack!" Vanessa's phone rang as she ran to grab it off her table. She was anxious to see who was calling. She prayed that it wasn't anyone who saw the eviction notice on her door.

It was late, and she wasn't expecting anyone to be calling.

She was happy to see the name of her friend, Gabrielle, on the caller I.D. She hadn't talked to Gabrielle in months and was surprised at the timing of the call. "Hey, girl," Vanessa answered. "You okay?"

Vanessa could hear the concern in her friend's voice. Vanessa thought about saying she was okay, but something inside of her gave her the strength to be honest. Vanessa told Gabrielle how far behind she was on all of her bills, how she hardly had enough money to eat or pay for electricity this month, and how she was now facing eviction from her apartment.

"I need some help. Can you lend me some money, just enough so I don't get kicked out?

I'm sorry to ask, but I don't know what else to do. I promise I will pay you back as soon as I can. I'll even pay you back interest if you want."

Vanessa was out of breath by the time she finished. She felt like the wind had been knocked out of her. This was the first time she had ever asked anybody for help, and the weight of that felt heavy on her shoulders.

Gabrielle was quiet on the other end of the phone. Vanessa could only listen to the loud pounding of her head and heart.

To ease her growing cotton mouth, Vanessa walked to the kitchen to get some water. Her mouth had never felt so dry; it was beginning to hurt every time she swallowed.

The silence broke as Gabrielle made Vanessa an offer.

"I'm going to ATL this weekend for a private party at this club. I've done a couple of jobs there before, there are some ballers in there waiting to make it rain. Why don't you come with me? I know if you do, you won't need to worry about money or bills or anything for a while.

girls were bringing home at least 5 bands a night!"

Vanessa walked over to her sofa and inhaled a deep breath. It had only been a year and a few months, but she had worked hard to leave dancing behind her. Even though the money would solve most of her problems, she had decided to give her life to Christ.

Vanessa went to grab her Bible for strength. She knew that she had to decline the offer, but the money kept talking to her. Dancing to get ahead of her bills seemed like the logical thing to do.

"One weekend could cover paying her rent and then some; it seemed like a no-brainer. Then the eviction notice appeared in her mind. She knew this is where her faith had to kick in.

"I can't be out dancing and doing that stuff anymore. I'm a believer now. I can't do it," she resisted.

"Oh, girl, Georgia is a whole different state.

Nobody would even know you there, and you know I won't tell anybody. Think of all the cash. You'd get paid immediately, and your little situation would be resolved. Plus, it would be fun to catch up with you. I miss you, girl."

Vanessa hesitated. "Let me think about it." "I'm not hanging up until you're done thinking. I'm going to wait on the phone with you until you decide."

Gabrielle turned her speakerphone on and set the phone down next to the stove where she was waiting for her curling iron to heat up.

"Ouch!" someone yelled on the other side of the phone.

"Who are you with?" Vanessa asked, annoyed to hear another voice in Gabrielle's background. She didn't want to have this conversation in front of strangers.

The subject should have been talked about in private.

Vanessa couldn't understand why Gabrielle would continue to talk about this with another person in the room.

"It's just my cousin. I think you met her before. I'm doing her hair. She keeps moving around and then has the nerve to get mad when she gets burned. Never mind her, are you coming with me? Don't try to change the subject." Gabrielle laughed for a brief moment. "If you do go, you'll have to pick me up. I don't have a car anymore."

Vanessa was becoming more and more irritated, but still couldn't shake the feeling that this was her only option. "I'll go with you, but I can't drive. My car has too many miles on it. I can ask my sister if we can use her car, but if not, we can just get a rental." Gabrielle let out her trademark excited squeal, and the two of them made plans to drive to the ATL Friday morning.

Vanessa hung up the phone feeling no better or worse than before. She opened her Bible, but quickly closed it, feeling ashamed about the agreement she made. She knew that God would not be happy with her decision, but she was determined to go anyway.

CHAPTER SIX

It's Just Business

Friday morning rolled around, and Vanessa overslept. She stumbled around her apartment as she began to pack, cursing herself for not starting the night before. It had been a while since she had done a job like this, so she had trouble finding all her necessary items.

When Vanessa pulled up to Gabrielle's house, she was already sitting outside, waiting. She arrived over an hour later than the time they had agreed upon. Without hesitation, Gabrielle jumped up and threw her bags into the trunk. One of the things Vanessa liked about Gabrielle was her cool-minded attitude. She was carefree and easygoing. Sometimes her people-pleasing attitude got her into some pretty uncomfortable - and even dangerous - situations, but her personality was still admired.

Vanessa and Gabrielle talked and laughed as they drove down the highway. They had not seen each other since Vanessa left the dancing scene. Gabrielle was one of the few girls she got along with from the club. Most of the other dancers were the jealous and untrustworthy type. The two caught up on everything that had happened since they had last seen each other. Guys they had gone out with and even some of the girls they used to know became the topic of discussion. Then, Gabrielle brought up the elephant in the room.

"So, what's this whole living for Christ thing? You serious, girl? Is that why you haven't been around?"

Vanessa smiled. She hoped Gabrielle would bring this up, as this transformation in her life was something she was extremely proud of.

Vanessa began to tell her story about her transformation. One morning, after a night of drinking and drugs, she woke up next to a man she didn't recognize.

As she tiptoed out of her room, she saw her cousin asleep on the sofa. Her cousin was always vocal about how they had always admired her, but Vanessa knew they had no idea how she made her living. Unaware of how she got to this place, shame filled her like never before, she came to herself as she recognized there had to be a more fulfilling way to make a living.

As she walked towards the corner store, she was approached by a man she hadn't seen in years. He was dressed in a fancy suit. She asked him, "Where are you going so early in the morning?"

"I'm on my way to church," he replied. "I've been going for a while now. God has truly transformed my life. I surrendered everything to Him."

Vanessa was amazed as she remembered how reckless he used to be.

"That's good to hear. That church has really changed you. I like this side of you."

Before she could comment on anything else, he boasted, "It wasn't the church. It was God. He grabbed my attention when I was in prison, and my life has been moving forward since. I'd like you to come with me; might do you some good."

Vanessa shook her head, quickly denying his offer. There was no way she could sit through an entire church service after what she had just experienced.

"I'm not proud of a lot of things in my life, and I probably should go, but today isn't the day." she said.

He nodded his head in understanding, then handed her a pamphlet with the worship schedule of his church and the different classes they offered. "Well, I hope to see you there some other time then." Vanessa took the pamphlet, threw it into her purse, and turned to walk into the store. A few days later, she saw him again, this time handing money to a less fortunate person. He was preaching to the guy about salvation.

As other people listened, they became curious and stopped to hear his message, and soon a crowd quickly formed.

She watched the people who began to surround him as she walked over to hear what he was saying. He spoke with so much wisdom. Witnessing what God had done in his life made her want to learn what it was like to walk with Him. She was amazed by what God had done. To think that was the same guy who used to beat up men that stood on corners begging for money. His speech made Vanessa decide she would give the church thing a try, and she hadn't turned back since.

"Okay, but what's so good about it? I just don't understand why we had to stop talking as much. I mean, you stopped picking up my calls and everything.

Do you feel like I'm beneath you and don't want to hang around me anymore?" Gabrielle questioned Vanessa after she finished her story.

Vanessa waited until they pulled up to a red light and turned her head to look Gabrielle in her eyes.

A moment of silence passed, and the tension grew between the ladies. Vanessa wasn't sure how her testimony turned into Gabrielle being beneath her. Turning away and choosing the view from the window, Gabrielle broke the silence first, "It sounds to me like you're turning into one of those judgmental church folks, and I don't like that. That's the main reason I don't go to church."

"Everybody thinks that they are better than the next person. We are all sinners." Vanessa shook her head and tried to find the words to explain that it was nothing personal. She had to get rid of certain distractions to grow spiritually.

The changes she made allowed her to feel more fulfilled and happier. It wasn't about being better than the next person or judging anybody else's actions; she only wanted to change her own lifestyle.

She added how everyone she met at church was everything but judgmental, and that they were some of the friendliest and most supportive people she had ever met.

"Oh; not judgmental? Mmmm. Tell them to go to that gay club. I forget the name of it, but you know how church folks hate gay people. You can't tell me those church folks don't be trying to send every gay person straight to hell; especially if they don't agree to change their lives instantly." Gabrielle emphasized.

With one hand on the steering wheel and the other holding her head, trying to keep it from pounding, Vanessa did her best to hold in her frustration. How could she possibly be this oblivious?

How did her decision to grow spiritually turn into a conversation about the LGBTQ community?

"They aren't judging people for being gay.

They are simply spreading the word. God only approves of sex between married men and women.

Anything else is a sin." Just like stealing, lying, and cheating on your spouse. It's all the same. We all believe in something. Why am I made to feel bad about what I believe?"

Gabrielle cut Vanessa off. "What happened to 'love your neighbor as yourself'? And why does it matter? I'm sure they have other things in their own lives to worry about than to be worrying about who somebody else is sleeping with. It's none of their business. People need to just mind their own business. I swear, it's this kind of stuff that makes me not want to go to church."

"Wow, I can't believe you found something wrong with Christians encouraging people to live a life free from sin," said Vanessa.

Her patience was wearing thin, so she tried to end the conversation before one of them said something hurtful that they didn't mean.

"No, don't try to change the subject. All of a sudden you're acting like this life is beneath you.

You talk like you think I'm beneath you, too. But you know what? There's only one of us in this car who is about to be homeless and can't pay their bills, and that person is not me."

"Where are your new church friends? Why aren't they helping you now?"

Gabrielle looked over to see Vanessa trying to force a smile with tears in her eyes. She immediately felt guilty about what she said.

With her chin quivering, Vanessa pulled over to the side of the road. She knew she shouldn't have come.

She had made so much progress, and now she felt as though she was breaking her promise to God. Her only friendship from her previous life was going down the drain.

Gabrielle allowed Vanessa a moment to compose herself as she stepped out of the car and walked down the side of the road. As she watched her friend pace, she began to wonder if she was wrong for what she said. Gabrielle got out of the car and followed Vanessa.

"I'm sorry, V. Come back. I was out of line; it's been a long trip, and we are both tired." Soon the Atlanta traffic started to pick up, and Vanessa didn't feel safe. Walking back to the car, the girls apologized and made up, and Vanessa agreed to continue driving.

The drive to the club was silent.

"We're here," Gabrielle said when they arrived. She pointed towards the back of the parking lot. "You can park over there."

People were already lined up a mile long to get inside. The strip club was well-lit and large, like a grand warehouse.

The girls grabbed their things and headed in. Before they reached the doors, Gabrielle apologized again, "Hey, I'm really sorry about what I said earlier. Are we still good?"

Vanessa looked at her and gave a half-hearted nod. She felt many emotions, but "good" was not one of them.

The two continued to walk into the strip club from the back entrance.

The dressing room was much bigger than the clubs Vanessa knew in Florida. The girls had their own showers and dressing rooms.

You could tell that a lot of money was coming in and out of the club. They did their makeup and put their outfits on, not saying a word to each other.

After she finished getting dressed, Vanessa looked at herself in the mirror. It felt like forever since she had worn such a skimpy outfit. She saw a version of herself that she had grown to hate.

She wanted to cover herself up and run away, but she knew it was too late for that now.

"Are you ready?" Gabrielle asked her friend glancing at Vanessa, before heading to walk towards the main club. Vanessa hesitantly followed behind. "This is all you. Own it, girl. We got bills to pay." The girls hugged, and Gabrielle went on her way. Taking in a deep breath, Vanessa reminded herself that this was only for one night and never again.

She soon found the group of men she would be entertaining for the night, walked over, and introduced herself, then began doing her thing.

Once the night started to wind down, Vanessa quickly bagged up her money. She felt filthy, and so did the money she was touching.

She couldn't wait for the night to end and leave this life forever for the second time. The shower was calling her name.

Vanessa was bent over; picking up some leftover hundreds off the floor to add to her earnings when one of the men from the group she was entertaining came over. He smiled, placed his hand on her bottom, and pulled her into him. Vanessa quickly pushed back.

"Come on, baby, I saw the way you were looking at me. Let's take this party back to my place."

Chills ran down her spine when he spoke to her. He was aggressive and knew nothing of personal space. It was as if he was challenging her to deny him.

"No thank you." She held her bag tighter and tried to walk away. It was normal for men to behave this way. It came with the territory. Some of them couldn't understand that the dancing and flirting were part of her job and nothing more. Before she could get a safe distance away from him, the man grabbed her arm and pulled her back.

She again tried to brush off his grasp and get away, but struggled as his grip on her arm became even tighter.

Vanessa was a petite woman, and even though she had a fierce personality, she was physically outmatched by this man, who had to be over a foot taller and more than a hundred pounds heavier than her.

"Leave me alone. I'm not going home with you. That little performance was just business. This is my job. It's all just a show."

The man wouldn't take no for an answer and started pulling her to a corner of the club.

Vanessa tried to yell for one of the other girls to help her, but the club was too loud, and the flashing lights made her hard to spot.

Everyone was too busy enjoying their night. They had no idea who Vanessa was or what was happening.

"You're mine tonight. Do you hear me?" The man angrily yelled in Vanessa's face, clearly more upset than he appeared minutes earlier. Despite the man's frustration, Vanessa continued to tightly grab her bag as he violently pulled her to the corner of the club. At this point, she had made it clear that she was not giving in to him that night.

With all his strength, he flung her down, causing her to tumble to the ground and hit her head against the wall. He quickly picked up her bag and disappeared into the crowd.

As they fought, only a single twenty-dollar bill remained in the bag. She picked it up, but the rest of her money was gone.

Twenty bucks was all she had to show for betraying her morals and her promise to God. Twenty dollars and a bump on her head. She ran to the ladies' room, found an empty stall, and cried.

CHAPTER SEVEN

A Close Call

Gabrielle agreed to do the driving on the way home. Vanessa was in no mood to focus on the road or engage in any small talk. She tried to sleep, but Gabrielle drove like a maniac. It felt as if the car was accelerating non-stop as Gabrielle swerved in and out of traffic. Vanessa grew irritated with her driver as she started to feel a bit car sick.

"Why are you driving all crazy?" Vanessa opened an eye to peek over at Gabrielle, who looked nervous and kept glancing in the rearview mirror.

"I'm trying to lose them. They've been following us for the last five miles."

Vanessa sat up quickly, not knowing who Gabrielle was talking about. Her first thought was one of the men from the club, but she saw something much more nerve-wracking when she looked behind her.

The flashing of blue and red sirens woke her up. Vanessa saw the look of panic on Gabrielle's face.

"You do have your license, don't you?" she asked. Gabrielle finally slowed down and pulled over to the side of the road, looking at Vanessa.

"I wouldn't be driving if I didn't. Please don't start with your better-than-everybody-else attitude. Like you're the only person around who has a license."

"Gabrielle," Vanessa sighed, "I know that you're frustrated, but we're going to be okay. Just do whatever they ask. I'm sure this is all a big misunderstanding."

Gabrielle shook her head and started crying. "No, V, you don't understand.

I wanted to tell you sooner, but you had so much going on that I didn't want to bother you with it.

I'm so sorry to tell you this now, but I've got a brick in my suitcase."

Vanessa stared at her in disbelief. "I bought it from one of the girls at the club.

But there's no need to worry, it's wrapped up good. My license is clear too, so they won't mess with us. Let's get this ticket and you can fuss at me later. I put it in the bottom of my suitcase. They're not going to find it. If we're not cool, we're both going to jail." Gabrielle finished her speech and turned to look ahead.

Vanessa softly began to cry, regretting not following her instincts. Gabrielle looked at her with pity.

"I'm so sorry for bringing you here and getting you involved.

I’m a horrible person, and I understand now why you stopped answering my calls. You deserve to have better people in your life. I'm a bad influence."

"You worked so hard to change, and I ruined everything for you. I'm so sorry."

She grabbed Vanessa's hand and squeezed it so tight that it was beginning to feel numb. Vanessa was scared and couldn't believe the situation she was in.

Why did she allow herself to get here? She looked in the rearview mirror and saw the officer approach their car. She began to pray.

"Heavenly Father, please deliver us from this situation. I confess that I messed up. I hear you speaking to me loud and clear. Please protect us, Lord, and command your angels to guard us, Lord. Forgive me, Lord, and give me the wisdom to do better. I ask that you deliver me from the consequences of the poor decisions that I've made. In Jesus' name, I pray."

Her prayer was interrupted by a knock on the driver's side window. Vanessa then looked out of her side window and saw another police car pulling up. Her stomach did a flip when she saw the second officer open the door of his SUV to bring out the dogs.

They were huge and more intimidating than either of the cops. She knew they didn't just bring dogs around for no reason. They had to have received a tip.

"Ma'am, I need to see your license and registration."

Vanessa opened the glove compartment, hoping her sister had kept the registration on her car current. Gabrielle got her license out of her wallet, her hand trembling as she handed it over to the officer. The officer with the dog walked around the car and mentioned something to the officer who had asked for Gabrielle's documents. The two walked back toward the car, one on each side of the vehicle.

"Step out of the vehicle; we're going to need to conduct a search."

Gabrielle let out an audible gasp. They looked at each other and unbuckled their seatbelts, then opened their doors. Gabrielle exited the car first. Vanessa slowly opened the door, and then stopped.

"You can't search the car without a warrant," she said to the officer. "During a traffic stop, warrants aren't required from a judge if we have probable cause," he replied. Vanessa tried to think of something to argue back at the officer, but her thoughts were interrupted by the barking dog that stood near the trunk of the car.

"And there it is. Probable cause."

The officer was stone-faced as he pointed toward the trunk. Vanessa stepped out of the vehicle.

The cop searched her and then walked back to see what the dogs had found.

Vanessa walked over next to Gabrielle and grabbed her hand and continued her prayer. This time she spoke louder and more convincingly.

“You told me to put my trust in you when I'm afraid. Your word says that you are a gracious God. You are greater than any person or anything. Have mercy on me, Lord. It's you that I trust; I will not be afraid. I'm trusting in you, Lord. I'm trusting in you, Amen.”

The cop that initially pulled the car over, began to search the trunk of the car. He first opened Vanessa’s luggage and rummaged around her belongings. He then moved on to Gabrielle’s. The dog began to bark louder.

He pulled her bag closer so he could look inside. When he realized what was inside, he took a long look over at Vanessa and Gabrielle, who were standing hand in hand.

The officer then zipped up the luggage and closed the trunk.

He turned and walked back over to the ladies. Vanessa closed her eyes, terrified of what was about to happen.

“We’re clear. They’re free to go.” The cop said to the other as he walked past them.

Vanessa opened her eyes. Gabrielle looked at her in disbelief. Did we hear him right? They both saw him look in the bag; he had to know what was inside.

However, the cop said nothing. He walked over to Gabrielle and returned her driver's license to her. Then he looked at Vanessa. They maintained eye contact for several moments. The intensity from the look in his eyes communicated that he was an honest and trustworthy man.

"Are you a believer?" he asked, looking in Vanessa's direction. She nodded her head quickly as Gabrielle looked in the opposite direction.

"Then walk like one." He turned to walk away. "Ladies, you're free to go. Have a good day."

Vanessa wanted to run over and hug him but calmly climbed back into the passenger seat again. After the officers left, the two friends hugged each other and cried with relief before continuing their drive home.

CHAPTER EIGHT

New Beginnings

Wood was suiting up for his first day as a security guard. The uniform had many pieces to it, and he wanted to make sure nothing was missing. This new job was the start of what would hopefully be the rest of his life. Looking at himself in the mirror, his mind flashed back to his earlier years. He used to give security guards so much trouble, and now here he was, about to be one.

Wood paced back and forth as he waited for his ride to pick him up. Since his car was still in the shop, Wood had to resort to any means possible to get around, at least whenever Ray wasn't able to take him places. The car finally arrived, and Wood was surprised to see a beautiful young woman in the driver's seat. Wood couldn't help but flirt with the driver, and she politely played along.

Wood continued to make small talk, asking her silly questions about how long she'd been driving and if she liked her job. The drive to work would only take about twenty minutes, so Wood made the best of it. "My shift is over at nine. You wanna give me your number so I can call you directly to pick me up? Maybe we can grab a bite to eat," he teased the driver. She turned up the music and ignored Wood's suggestion. He tried again, "Come on, I promise I'll be a gentleman. I just want to get to know you better." The driver smiled and shook her head, keeping her eyes on the road. Wood laughed and settled back into his seat, enjoying the rest of the ride to work.

"I'll be pretty hungry by then, and I'd like you to join me for dinner." This time, the driver turned around and snapped, "I don't go out with grown men who don't have their own ride."

Wood couldn't believe how rude she was acting. They sat in silence as they approached his destination.

Before he left, Wood had some advice to give before stepping out of the car.

"You know, you should never judge a book by its cover. I was in an accident recently, and now my car is in the shop." Before she could respond, Wood gave a tight smile and started his way to the building. He didn't even bother to look back at the driver but hoped she would take what he said to heart.

Once inside, Wood met up with the shift trainer, who handed him a massive stack of paperwork to fill out. Wood had never had a job that required paperwork before, so he was a little overwhelmed just looking at it. Lucky for him, the trainer got a call about a regular shoplifter back in the store.

"Leave the paperwork for later. Now it's time to see what you're made of. Let the training begin."

Wood followed along, excited to put the paperwork down.

"The call said the shoplifter was wearing an oversized black hoodie and carrying a bag from another store."

Wood spotted the guy first and pointed him out so his trainer would see him. "Alright, we're going to approach him but try not to cause a commotion. Let's try to take him to the back office because we don't need to search him out here in the open."

Wood nodded at his trainer and followed closely, neither saying a word to each other. The trainer got to the shoplifter first and grabbed his arm. The man did not struggle as the trainer led him to the back office.

As they walked the culprit to the back, a voice from their walkie-talkies spoke. "Where are you at? The shoplifter is heading toward the purse section near the exit. Get over there now."

Wood and the trainer looked at each other with surprise. The trainer apologized to the guy they had in hand who luckily did not cause a scene.

The trainer spotted the actual shoplifter and headed in his direction.

The shoplifter made eye contact with him as he approached; dropped the bag he had filled with stolen merchandise and ran out of the store.

CHAPTER NINE

Back On The Outside

The industrial gated doors opened, and Todd took his first steps out. He was finally a free man. He had confessed earlier to his bunker, John, that he would be returning to his street life once he got out because he had nowhere else to go. Todd had been in for years and no longer had the resources he needed to jump back into the game.

John knew the game all too well; he was a heroin kingpin before getting locked up. However, he still had connections and communicated with the outside world regularly. Before he left, John tried to convince Todd to try a different way of living so that he wouldn't end up back in prison, but Todd wasn't hearing no advice. Instead, he walked John down memory lane, recalling all the favors he had done for him while they had been locked up.

John hesitated, "Hey, if you insist on going through with it, you gotta find Wood. He's an OG in the game and will look out for you. Wood owes me a favor anyway. Let him know that I sent you. I'm sure you two will cross paths. He'll take care of you."

Todd took note of the name and agreed. He knew he probably would not see John again once he was released. John swore off the street life years ago after serving 27 years for a crime he didn't commit.

Outside, Todd went back to the old area where he was introduced to Ray. The two decided to work together. Todd ran errands with Ray, meeting new people and learning the new ways of the streets. Things hadn't changed too much while he was away. On one of their runs, Ray mentioned that he had to check on a friend. Todd looked out the window and noticed a tall, slim guy walking toward the car. He felt like he knew him from somewhere but wasn't sure. Everybody looked like someone out here.

"Yo, Todd. This is my boy, Wood."

Todd chuckled to himself. Of course, it was Wood. He didn't think the two would meet so soon.

"Wood just got a pool hall. Come inside with me to check it out," Ray said, sounding so excited. Todd agreed.

Todd turned to face Wood, "Hey, I'm Todd. I'm a friend of John's. He said you'd know the name."

Wood's eyes enlarged, and he wasn't sure what to say. He hadn't heard that name in years and hoped he never would again.

"Yeah, yeah, I know John. How's he doing?" "What do you think?" Todd was put off by Wood's arrogant question.

Wood didn't mean to come off like that; he was just shocked and wasn't expecting to meet someone who knew John. Especially sitting in Ray's car.

"Who's John?" Ray asked, unaware of their mutual connection. "Itt's a long story." Wood said. "Let's just say John was an acquaintance of Wood's. Sound about right?" Todd asked.

Wood nodded his head and hoped they would leave it at that. He felt horrible knowing that John was doing time for a crime that he committed. He made a mental note to write to him and send him some money.

Inside the pool hall, Wood nervously started reorganizing things, trying to avoid any conversation with Todd. Ray looked around and smiled. "This is nice, man!"

Ray ran around the pool hall like a child, trying to take in everything at once. He had been inside the same pool hall many times when Antonio was the owner, but now that it belonged to Wood, it seemed completely different. Antonio had let the place go. Wood had put so much time and effort into cleaning the place up.

There was graffiti art, colorful carpet, and he even added an arcade room. It looked like the perfect place for some innocent fun

Wood smiled as a group of kids from the block came into the hall. They were a loud bunch, excited to see Wood. These kids would come in almost every day; some of them even helped Wood get the place back in order. He let them paint and make small repairs. He hoped they would learn some life lessons while they were at the pool hall and stay away from the street life. Wood also liked to lead them in prayer whenever they came to see him. He called the kids over, and they all listened as he recited scripture after scripture. There was a fifty-dollar reward waiting for the kid who remembered the longest scripture. "Romans 12:2 says, 'Do not be conformed to this world, but be transformed by the renewing of your mind." Wood said. "Now, go play some pool." He dismissed the kids, allowing the boys to stay as long as they wanted.

Wood knew most of them had no other safe place to go. They definitely reminded him of himself when he was younger.

Wood wished he had a safe place to go with his friends at their age instead of getting mixed up in the game. Ray looked at his friend in awe. Even though he had always looked up to and respected Wood, he now saw him in a whole new light. Wood kept talking about how he was turning his life around, but this was the first time Ray could visibly see the change. He was happy for Wood.

CHAPTER TEN

Telling His Story

Vanessa saw Wood sitting by himself at the singles meeting. He hadn't been to one of the meetings in the past two weeks, and she was happy to see him. She waved and headed over to him. She said, "Nice to see you. Where have you been?" Wood told Vanessa all about his pool hall and the time, work, and money he had put into it. Wood beamed with pride as he talked about the pool hall becoming a place for the kids on the block to hang out and how he wanted to help them stay out of trouble. "The kids were reluctant to hear me preach at first, but after I offered them money, they started asking to lead the prayers. You know, money changes a joker real quick. Jokers be like, 'What do you want a joker to do?'"

The two laughed. "That's amazing, Wood.

You're doing good things for those kids. Speaking of good things, I'm going to see my brother next week.

He's at the state prison about an hour away. Why don't you come with me? Those guys need to hear how somebody like you turned into the successful entrepreneur that you are today. You never know who you could inspire." Wood was a little hesitant but agreed. He didn't know how to say no to Vanessa. The two agreed to just be friends, even though he loved spending time with her. As they made the hour-long drive to the prison, Vanessa could tell Wood was nervous and reassured him that he would do fine. During the ride he asked if he could practice the speech he had prepared.

"You don't need some speech. Just tell your story, from the heart," she encouraged. Wood nodded and took a deep breath. Vanessa changed the subject to something lighter, hoping that it would help Wood relax. The two of them talked and laughed for the rest of the drive.

The security process went by pretty quickly. Their IDs and belongings were scanned. Vanessa left her car keys and wallet in a locker, and they were escorted into a room where the inmates were visiting with their families. Vanessa ran to her brother and hugged him. She introduced him to Wood, and the three began to talk. Vanessa told her brother about meeting Wood at church and how he was helping her turn her life around. Her brother thanked Wood and expressed his gratitude as well as his sorrow for not being there to protect his sisters anymore.

He told Wood stories about how he used to walk Vanessa home from work some nights so that none of the guys would try to follow her home from the club. He was so glad she wasn't doing any of that stuff anymore, but he still worried about her.

Vanessa held on to her brother's hand as he spoke. She always adored her brother and having him away for so long had been challenging for her.

After he went away, the rest of her family grew apart, and she missed the life they knew before.

A prison guard called Wood over to be led into the meeting room where some of the inmates had gathered to hear him speak. Wood looked back at Vanessa, who again assured him he would be great. Wood followed the guard and left Vanessa and her brother to catch up. He took a big gulp and looked at the small crowd gathered in the meeting room.

Most of the inmates were younger than him. Wood's heart went out to them. They could have done anything with their lives, but due to a couple of wrong turns, they were here. He remembered being where they were. Being back in this place reminded him of the little trouble he got in years ago.

It caused him to feel something he hadn't felt in a long time. He wasn't sure what it was, but he knew he didn't like it.

Wood started his story from the beginning. He talked about growing up in Jacksonville with his parents who were good people and worked hard to provide for him and his siblings. During his speech, he mentioned that at some point, he hooked up with the wrong crowd and ended up leading that same crowd. Wood talked about how he gained respect after his first transaction. It made him one of the most successful street hustlers on the block. Each transaction made him feel more invincible. At one point, he was bringing in thousands of dollars a day.

After Wood was released from the halfway house, he tried to find honest work, but his friends kept pulling him back into the game. His record was cleared, so things weren't so hard. Knowing that he was barely making money made it easy to get back out there.

The money was his drug of choice. The streets were flooded with young guys hustling.

It didn't even feel bad being out there, that's until trouble showed up. Trust me, he will show up.

After being shot the second time, he realized how dangerous it all was.

The streets weren't worth his life. His cousin was shot and killed in front of him. A couple of his friends were also shot and killed over some alleged gang retaliation. Wood said he would take it all back if he could. The money, the reputation, none of it was worth the loved ones that he lost. He was near death himself, but God wasn't ready for him to go yet.

He recalled his parents tearfully at his bedside, praying for him and wondering where they went wrong. Wood mentioned Pastor Williams visiting him when he was at his weakest. Then, somewhere in the space between life and death, Wood called out for God to give him one more chance. He promised he would change his ways if God directed his path.

He was too young to die, and there was so much that he didn't get to do.

In the days that followed, Wood began to recover. The nurses at the hospital were amazed.

More people joined the group to listen to Wood's story.

"It didn't happen overnight, and I struggled with leaving my old life behind. I was tempted to return to my old ways, but through prayer, I was able to find strength."

The inmates listened intently, many of whom had lived similar lives as Wood's. They had been locked up for similar reasons and had suffered losses due to gang violence.

Wood encouraged them to break free from their circumstances and commit their lives to God, just as he had done. He offered his support and belief in them, saying,

"I believe in you, and I'll be here for you if you need me."

After his testimony, he invited any questions, and a voice from the crowd asked, "Can you pray for us?" Wood wasn't sure who made the request, but there was no way he would turn that request down.

Wood eagerly agreed, saying: "Bow your heads, please. Almighty God, Our Maker, Defender, Redeemer, and Friend. I ask you to help these young men find the strength within themselves to live a life that will lead them closer to you. Have Mercy and bless them with wisdom. Forgive them for their sins.

You said if we confess our sins, that you would forgive our sins and cleanse us from all unrighteousness. I'm asking that you be present and speak to those who diligently seek your presence." On the drive home, Wood told Vanessa how things went and how he hoped that his words touched at least one of the men in that room.

After hearing his experience, Vanessa shed a tear. She was so proud of the growth that she saw in her friend.

CHAPTER ELEVEN

An Unexpected Opportunity

"Wood, can I talk to you for a minute?" Wood's heartbeat sped up as he was taken by surprise to see Pastor Williams enter the pool hall. Taking a step back, Wood was at a loss for words. The Pastor had never visited him before. Wood was happy to see him nonetheless. Pastor Williams informed Wood that he had heard about his testimony at the prison a few days earlier from one of the inmates he kept in touch with.

"You have a gift, you know that? There's a pastor down the way who is not doing so well. I would love for you to come with me to visit him." Pastor Williams continued, "I'm sure he could use some company. His story is almost the same as yours, son. He was able to influence others just like you. He might be your brother," Pastor Williams urged. He watched Wood contemplate his offer and hoped he would accept the invitation.

Growing up on the streets, Wood struggled to find himself like everyone else. But being in that environment taught him many valuable lessons. One thing he knew for sure was that he had a gift for influencing people to get what he wanted. When he was younger, he remembered watching police officers conduct raids that took dozens of dealers off the streets.

He used his influence to recruit younger guys from his hood to willingly take their place. In his old life as a supplier, trust was essential. He needed someone to move his product, and the last thing he wanted to do was trust a stranger he didn't know from Jack. Replacing the ones who got caught with new kids from the block made sense to him. Convincing them to follow his lead was a piece of cake. Evaluating the powerful influences who helped him overcome his many challenges to shape the life he has now, he only wanted to spread to others what was given to him.

There were so many lives he had ruined, so it only seemed right. "We need good folks out here; that's why I'm putting these kids on. Adults are hardheaded, Pastor. I know you. It's hard running a business. I can only imagine the stuff you have to deal with, doing church business while leading a church." Pastor Williams laughed, "We are all still learning and improving. It's a never-ending journey. I'm convinced that God is just as concerned about your growth as he is with the churches. I'm on my way to see him now, do you have some time to join me? I won't keep you long."

Wood agreed and the two made the quick drive to see the sick pastor.

Before he could get his nerves together the Pastor pulled into a neighboring hospice facility. Wood was a little taken aback.

He hadn't realized the pastor was sick enough to be in hospice. Wood was overcome with a sense of anxiety.

The two parked and began walking toward the front entrance.

"Who are you here to see?" The nurse asked as she opened the door. Pastor Williams gave the name, and she smiled as they were instructed to follow her.

"The pastor has been sleeping for most of the day, but you're welcome to stay as long as you like. I'm sure that he'll be happy to see you." She pointed to the room where he was staying and both men walked in.

Wood felt his stomach drop when he saw the pastor sleeping peacefully in his bed.

He couldn't tell if the poor guy was dead or alive. Walking over to the bed, he put his hand on the pastor's shoulder in a gentle manner.

The pastor's eyes opened, and Wood watched as he took what seemed an immense amount of energy to speak. Each word and breath he took seemed like a struggle.

"I'm so glad to see you," he finally whispered. His voice was faint and weak. Pastor Williams introduced Wood to the sick Pastor.

Pastor Williams filled him in on Wood's past and how he had promised to devote the rest of his life to God. Wood then brought him up to speed on what he was doing lately with the pool hall and about the kids who looked up to him so much.

Pastor Williams told him about how Wood made a positive impact on the inmates the time he went out to encourage them. Wood smiled as he was starting to realize that his life was changing right before his eyes.

He had been too busy for it all to truly sink in, but it did; it hit him at that moment. All he could do was smile.

After intently listening, the ailing pastor visibly strained to sit up and look Wood directly in the eyes. He then lifted a shaky finger and pointed at Wood.

You are the type of man I am looking for. I spent my life trying to make an impact in our community. God used me to bring several people to Him, and I know how many more lives need to be saved out there. If you have been blessed with the power of influence, that's exactly what the church needs. God said it's time, son. It's time."

Wood could only stand there, speechless. With nervousness yet interest in his voice, Wood said, "Pastor, I appreciate the kind words, but I can't take any credit for what God has done. Besides, I never thought about leading a church.

I just took on the responsibility of the pool hall, and I'm not sure how I could find the time... but I'll still help with what I can.

CHAPTER TWELVE

We Can't Escape The Past

Wood was pulling down some stools from the counter and setting up for another day at the pool hall. It was still early in the afternoon, so he didn't expect anyone to arrive for a few more hours. As he was wiping down the last stool, he heard the door's bells jingle.

"Hey, man, I could use some help," said a frantic but familiar voice. Wood saw Charlie standing in the doorway. He hadn't seen him since the night of his car accident and didn't even know that Charlie knew where to find him.

"Man, the block is hot, and the cops are on me. I need a place to lay low," Charlie pleaded.

Wood immediately shook his head.

The last thing he wanted was a known hustler hanging around his pool hall, selling drugs.

"I told you, I'm not in the game anymore. I've started a new life. I'm living for God now and want nothing to do with that street life. You'll have to lay low on the other side of that door. Not here. Nope, not happening."

Wood could tell Charlie didn't like his answer. He could sense the raw anger steaming from him as he started walking closer towards Wood, but Wood remained unfazed. "Man, I helped you when you needed it, and this is the thanks I get?" Charlie yelled.

Wood turned away and shook his head in utter disbelief. *'If I knew Charlie would expect to be repaid for giving me a ride, I might as well have accepted the cash offer.* That cash would have made things a whole lot easier for me," Wood thought to himself. Between Charlie and Todd, Wood knew that leaving his old life behind was going to be more challenging than he imagined.

He felt like he owed everyone at least a favor or two. John was going to be released soon, and he could only imagine what he had up his sleeve.

In the following weeks, it was inevitable that the pool hall became a hot spot. Charlie and a couple of his boys were always there, working. Wood tried his hardest to keep the kids from seeing it. After 6 pm, the street cats flowed in and out of the pool hall like clockwork. Very few actually played pool. Soon, Charlie started acting like the place was his own.

While helping a kid with his math homework, the kid nodded toward Charlie who was clearly engaged in a transaction with another person. Wood tried to brush it off and get the kid back to his work.

"So, you know how to solve this problem, right?"

Wood asked, hoping to snap the kid back into focus.

"You know what they're doing, right?" the kid asked in return, looking Wood straight in the eye.

Wood shook his head and shrugged, pretending to be clueless. He didn't feel like much of a leader lately and didn't know how to make things stop without risking everything. The kid wasn't letting up, so Wood gave in.

"That right there is an example of everything having a cause and effect. Things have a way of coming back to bite you dead in your butt, and there ain't nothing you can do about it but watch it all play out. This is one of those times, kid. Just make sure you never end up making those types of moves. I promise you that it won't end well." He then got up and left the kid to his work at the table, desperately wishing he could take his own advice.

CHAPTER THIRTEEN

From Bad To Worse

On a Thursday evening, Vanessa and a friend from church were playing a round of pool. She enjoyed coming to the pool hall to support her friend and felt safe there because it allowed her to take her mind off all her responsibilities. Wood noticed the ladies and walked over to thank them for stopping by.

While they were talking, Vanessa noticed a group of guys enter and head straight to the back of the building. She recognized one of them and knew he was trouble. They sat down near a pool table, but it was clear they had no intention of playing. Vanessa tapped Wood to get his attention.

She pointed to the men, "Wood, this isn't good. You don't need this going on in here." Vanessa was worried that maybe Wood had given up on his promise to God and had something to do with what was going on.

Just as quickly as the thought popped into her head, the look of disappointment and concern that appeared on Wood's face as he watched the men, he told her things were not always as they appeared to be. Wood excused himself and quickly walked to the restroom. He felt like his chest was tightening, and the walls were closing in on him. He checked to see if anyone else was there and was relieved to find himself alone. Wood locked the door and splashed his face with cold water, hoping to feel more alert. He was trapped in a never-ending nightmare that he couldn't escape from. Taking a deep breath, he began to pray: "Heavenly Father, I'm trying to keep my promise. I'm submitting to you, Lord. Set me free from the devil, in Jesus' name. Make him flee, Lord. Make him flee!" Wood's breathing quickened, and he cried out, "Jesus, Jesus, Jesus!"

Wood's vision began to blur, and the tears started flowing. No matter how many deep breaths he took, he couldn't seem to fill his lungs with enough air.

Wood's emotions were all over the place. Feeling like a complete failure, Wood let out his frustration by punching the brick wall multiple times. Soon, he could function again. As the adrenaline rush slowed down, he wiped his tears and rubbed his bruised knuckles feeling the stinging sensation. Wood splashed water on his face, rolled his shoulders back, calmed himself down, and headed back out into the pool hall.

Wood walked straight over to the group of guys without hesitation. He made sure to place his gun in a spot on his waist where they could see it. He calmly asked them to leave.

Wood didn't want to cause a scene, but he also wanted to make his point clear.

The guys looked at Wood, then shrugged him off and continued their conversation, ignoring Wood's request. But Wood was not having the disrespect. "Look, you're operating openly and recklessly. People are talking.

I tried to let it slide, but I can't have that here. Keep all the money that you've made, but leave now, without making a scene." Wood repeated calmly, despite the intense anger burning inside.

Now he got their attention.

"You trippin' man. Leave us alone; we not bothering nobody," said one of the guys who tried to get aggressive with Wood. He began to walk towards Wood but was held back by one of the others.

Vanessa heard the commotion and became worried.

She pulled her phone out of her bag and watched the confrontation closely.

"Listen, you're leaving here one way or another," Wood said, hand on gun, eyes fixed on the guy who tried to walk up on him.

After a heated exchange, the group finally left, one glancing up at the ceiling cameras and warning Wood,

"You messed up, man" Wood knew that was intended to be a threat and felt his stomach drop.

It didn't feel good knowing that trouble was on the horizon and that someone could potentially get hurt. He played it off and took the small victory, happy for now; that they were out of the pool hall. The others continued hanging out and enjoying their time at the pool hall without any concerns.

Vanessa stepped outside and called the police, letting them know about the pool hall's disturbance. She was worried things would escalate, and Wood would end up hurt. Vanessa felt relieved as the group of guys walked out and continued down the street.

CHAPTER FOURTEEN

Revenge

Todd was smoking a cigarette outside the pool hall when the police arrived. They approached him with questions, one officer standing uncomfortably close to Todd's face.

"We heard there was a disturbance here. Know anything about that?" the cop asked. Todd shook his head, valuing his personal space.

“Meeting someone?” the cop continued.

Todd again shook his head. He didn’t like cops and wished they would leave him alone. They then asked Todd for identification. Todd refused, but after some resistance, Todd eventually got out his driver’s license for the cops to run.

"You're clear," said one of the cops, as he handed the license back to Todd and continued to question the others nearby.

Todd looked inside the pool hall where he saw Wood talking to Vanessa and shook his head. He could not believe that Wood would be foolish enough to get the police involved. Wood knew what happened to snitches. "I can't stand that dude." Todd said to another guy. He put out his cigarette and left.

Inside, everyone had calmed down from the earlier events, and Wood reassured Vanessa that she had done the right thing by calling the police. He thanked her for looking out for him.

Soon after, Vanessa and her friend headed home, and Wood locked up the pool hall. He walked back to his office, relieved to finally have a moment of peace. Wood reached for his phone, which had been in his office all evening, and saw 6 missed calls from Ray in quick succession.

He immediately called Ray's phone, only for it to be picked up by an unfamiliar woman.

"There's been an accident. It's not good."

Wood grabbed his things and rushed out the door, his heart racing with concern.

CHAPTER FIFTEEN

Lesson Learned

As soon as Wood arrived at the hospital, he rushed to Ray's bedside. Ray was in bad shape but still conscious and aware of Wood's presence. Before Ray could say anything, Wood began a prayer:

"Heavenly Father, I pray for my friend Ray. I ask you to heal him and keep him safe. Please protect him from evil. Amen."

Ray remained quiet, and then proceeded to tell Wood about the accident. He was driving to the pool hall when a car full of guys started trailing him, one brandishing a gun. Ray didn't know why they targeted him, but he tried to escape. The chase ended with Ray's car flipping off the road. He woke up in the hospital with no memory of the driver or car.

Wood's heart sank, suspecting the guys he confronted at the pool hall. They were trying to kill Ray to get back at him.

Wood filled Ray in on the pool hall incident, tears welling up as he finished the story. He never wanted Ray involved in this.

“It’s not your fault, man. You did what you had to do. I’m gonna be okay. Don’t blame yourself. Go home and get some sleep,” Ray said, trying to comfort his friend. “Look, I will probably need you to pick me up tomorrow when I get out of here. I don’t have a car anymore.”

Wood nodded while Ray chuckled at himself. Leave it to Ray to try to crack jokes while lying in a hospital bed. “Once, I pick you up, we are going straight over to the church,” said Wood. Ray groaned with annoyance and rolled his eyes. He motioned for Wood to leave by waving his hand, and Wood smiled.

At least that wasn’t a no. As Wood got up to leave his friend’s side, two police officers knocked on the door. “We’d like to ask you a few questions about your accident.”

The jolly atmosphere that was building quickly crashed when the sudden reminder of why they were there in the first place came back. Ray nodded his head in agreement, and the officers stepped inside the room.

“You want me to stay?” Wood asked.

Ray shook his head no, and Wood continued walking out the door. As he walked down the hospital hallways, all he could think about was how thankful he was to see that Ray would be okay. Wood couldn't bear the thought of losing another person close to him.

CHAPTER SIXTEEN

Life Without a Conscience

Some kids from the block helped sweep up the pool hall while Wood counted the cash register, preparing for a bank deposit. The kids said goodnight to Wood and gathered their belongings to leave for the night.

As they left, one turned back, saying, "Wood, come here! That's the guy that got Ray." Wood snapped to attention, his anger surging as he approached the front door. The kids had witnessed the car chase's start while walking home. Wood hesitated, unsure what to do when faced with Ray's attacker. The kid pointed to the guy standing down the street. "Call the police?" Wood took a long look, then replied, "No, kids. I've got this." The kids nodded and left.

Wood stepped outside; his rage almost uncontainable as he approached the perpetrator who put his friend in the hospital. "What are you doing here?" Wood almost screamed at Todd. "Meeting someone. Handling my business. You understand, being a businessman yourself," Todd replied nonchalantly, as if Wood were crazy.

"Why here, man? I'm trying to run a business and create a clean safe space for the hood. Kids and churchgoers come here. I don't want them to see this. It's bad enough that they see it in their neighborhoods. I'm trying to create a safe environment and build a better community without this stuff. You know what I'm saying?"

Todd brushed off Wood: "I don't care. It's safe for me, that's all that matters. Plus, you owe John a favor. He said you'd look out for me, so chill."

Wood looked at Todd in disbelief, not sure what to say. Todd had neither fear nor remorse in his eyes.

At least after all the dirt Wood did in his past, he still had a conscience. He wasn't so sure that was the same for anybody anymore. Tired with giving in and annoyed for feeling like he had to, Wood had enough of Todd's threats.

"Listen, what happened with John was terrible, but I didn't ask him to do that bid for me. He did that on his own. He knew I was meant to be something greater, and I'm trying to be greater. Now you're getting in the way of that. Find somewhere else to make your money, and this is the last time I'm telling you that. God has given me a second chance to make something of myself, and I'm going to do that by any means necessary."

"Save that God-talk for someone else," Todd snapped. "There's a lot of money out here. I'm going to get all of it by any means necessary, so do what you gotta do. I'm not going anywhere."

Just then, a man Wood didn't recognize began walking toward them.

Wood didn't want any part of what was about to go down, so he turned and walked away. As he reentered the pool hall, he noticed a car sitting in an alley across the street from where Todd was standing. As soon as Todd accepted the money to complete the transaction, the car's lights flashed red, and four other vehicles pulled up. The man who had met Todd saw them first and took off running. In his rush to get away, he dropped the bag he had received from Todd.

"Hey! Stop right there!" two of the police officers yelled at the runner as they chased after him. Two cars stopped right in front of Todd. The door swung open and one of the cops jumped out. Todd was in handcuffs before he could even realize what was happening. He looked toward the pool hall, giving Wood one last stare before he went back to prison.

As he stepped back into the Prison gates, Todd couldn't believe he was back so soon.

If Wood hadn't set me up, I wouldn't be here anyway. The intrusion began as the guards conducted a body cavity search. Todd and the rest of the new inmates were stripped naked and given an orange jumpsuit, not caring about fit or comfort. The Dollar Store sandals made things that much more uncomfortable. Not to mention no new underwear or socks. The guard placed ankle shackles and chains around their waist, which connected to their handcuffs. Todd hated to hear the chains scrape against the floor once again as he dragged his feet toward the bus loading area.

The ride on the bus took hours, or at least it felt that way. The bus drove to other prisons to pick up more passengers, making the bus even more crowded until every seat was filled. The bus was filled with silence as no one uttered a single word.

The lack of air conditioning along with a few cracked windows on the bus was a recipe for an extremely hot and uncomfortable ride during the humid Florida summer.

Finally, the bus arrived at its final destination and the men walked in a line toward a door.

“Back so soon?” said a familiar voice.

Todd didn't have to turn to know who was speaking to him. John stood to the far right of Todd.

CHAPTER SEVENTEEN

I Hear You

Wood was running late when he spotted a couple of kids from the pool hall, dressed in their Sunday Best, talking to one of Charlie's boys. He slammed on his brakes and stopped in front of them.

"What are you all doing?" he asked.

The kids, recognizing Wood, ran to him with excitement, while Charlie's boy walked away.

"We were asking for money to pay our tithes at church. My momma says I can't go without paying," one kid explained.

Wood relaxed; relieved they were going to church, not getting involved in the streets.

"That nice man gave us each two five-dollar bills," another kid added.

Wood smiled, offering them a ride.

The kids excitement was contagious as they jumped into the car. When they arrived, the church was bustling with people. Wood felt happy to see the kids enthusiasm as they all stepped out of the vehicle.

"Can we sit up there?" one of the boys asked, pointing to an almost empty row in the middle of the church.

"Of course," Wood replied, and they made their way to their seats.

Soon after, the music started playing. Wood enjoyed the blend of Christian message and secular sound, which prompted most of the congregation to stand and dance along. "Sidestep, clap. Sidestep, clap," one boy said, studying the choir's dance moves aloud as others moved naturally to the beat. "Forward, hop. Side, hop.

Ahh, whatever. This too hard," he said, struggling to follow.

"No, it's not," another boy replied, standing up to join in. He quickly mastered the routine, copying the moves as if he'd been doing it for years. The other boys hesitated, then stood up to try dancing along, but they were turning into each other and kicking at the wrong time. The song ended, and everyone was asked to take their seats.

"Man, I'm tired. I need water. See a fountain?" one boy said.

The others were too busy getting peppermint candy from a woman next to them:

"Can I have one, please?" with an outstretched hand.

Vanessa stepped up to the podium and addressed the church. She had taken on the role to welcome the new members and teach the singles class every other Thursday.

"I want to extend a warm welcome to our first-time visitors. If you're visiting for the first time, please stand."

The boys hesitated to stand, but they did. They looked around and noticed quite a few other people were standing as well. Some were older, some younger, but all of them had the same apprehensive look on their face while the rest of the churchgoers looked at them and applauded.

"We're delighted to have you here. After the service, please visit our welcome center for a bag of homemade cookies made especially for you."

"Cookies!" one boy exclaimed loudly, prompting chuckles from nearby churchgoers.

A friend gave him a playful shove, whispering "be cool."

"What's your name?" a lady asked. "I'm Ralph, and these are my friends Curtis, Sam, and Darnel.

Nice to meet you, ma'am,"

Ralph greeted the nearby parishioners with a handshake, enjoying their connection. Their attention returned to the podium as the pastor spoke:

"Good morning! I'm thrilled to see you all today.

Before I get started on today's sermon, I would like to welcome a very special friend of mine that traveled from Detroit, Michigan to be here today. I want you to give it up for Mr. E. Thomas."

The church erupted in applause as Mr. Thomas walked forward and took his place behind the podium.

Mr. Thomas thanked the church and proceeded to share with the congregation his life story. He spoke about growing up in Detroit, while being raised by his mother who was a teenager when he was born. The two argued all the time.

There was no positive male figure involved,

so he dropped out of high school at an early age. Shortly after that, he became homeless. Being raised by the streets caused him to stay in trouble. He constantly found himself in situations where he had to prove himself.

One of his dearest friends had taken him off the streets and provided him with a safe place to stay. As he became comfortable, his dearest friend was shot in the head in front of him. Being a witness to the crime, the guy put a gun to his head. If it wasn't for a neighbor, he would have lost his life that night too.

Traumatized by the event, there were nights that he didn't get any sleep.

He reached his lowest point. His mother was in prison, and he had no person to turn to. Sleeping under the city bridge became most comfortable after midnight. Regulars often came out and offered him money or a place to shower.

However, there were days that he didn't have a drop to eat. He once went 3 days without food.

The times his grandmother prayed with him ran across his mind. She had gone to be with the Lord, but that third day of no food reminded him to pray.

"Growth doesn't come easy. Remember that.

You need to be strong and brave if you want to commit to leaving your old life behind.

You must put in work every single day. I believe in you, and I am here walking beside you. We will all grow together.

Let's walk together and help one another, church. You never know what your neighbor is going through." The church gave E. Thomas a very enthusiastic standing ovation as he ended his speech.

The choir began to sing, and collection trays were passed around.

The boys were excited to pull out their money, but Darnell noticed Ralph only put in $5.

"Hey man, I see what you did. Put that other five in there!" Ralph groaned, embarrassed he was caught trying to pocket the other five dollars.

The two boys laughed as they passed the tray to the next row. The congregation took their seats as the choir ended their song. Wood approached the podium to deliver his sermon.

He took a moment to take in the crowd before beginning his sermon. His greatest joy came from speaking to his community.

He now knew he made the right decision by accepting the responsibility to lead this church. He was still struggling to manage his and couldn't guarantee a special message at each service but was willing to learn and allow Christ to lead his footsteps. There was no denying that this was his calling.

It had only been a couple of months, but everyone approached him with so much love. He remembered one of the older ladies confessed to Wood that her grandson was ready for church before she was. They laughed together as Wood gave the young boy a high five.

“Let’s open our Bibles to II Corinthians 3:18."

One of the older ladies near the boys opened her Bible and handed it to the boys to share.

“Today's sermon will be about the secret of growth.” The sermon lasted for almost thirty minutes. Wood was pleased the crowd was engaged the entire time. “It's time for you to take responsibility for your growth.

We all made mistakes, so don't judge your neighbor, but encourage them. God doesn't want any of us to perish, he wants us to preach the gospel. I don't think you're hearing me, church."

Everyone turned around as he slowly made his way toward the front with the help of his cane. Being from the streets, he had gotten used to being in front of new people. Ray approached the pulpit; he closed his eyes.

Raising both hands in the air he announced to the congregation, "I hear you, and I'm ready. I want to give my life to Christ."

With his knees slightly bent and his head bowed down, he stood in front of the congregation with no shame. The crowd erupted in praise as they walked up to surround him with love.

Tears began to fall from his eyes as Ray's face became visible.

"God is good," Wood said. He stood back and allowed his friend to receive all that God had in store for him. It was starting to become common for young men to surrender their lives to Christ after Wood's services that never stopped the congregation from being friendly.

They were less concerned with the timing, and only wanted to show genuine love to everyone that entered the house of God.

Wood walked up to greet his friend with tears in his eyes. "It's about time." Ray wrapped his arms around Wood, "I'm so proud of you, brother. I'm so proud." The two hugged and began to cry together as the choir and music continued to play, filling the room with joy.

Ray laughed, "After everything that we've been through, we can finally say that we are blessed, too."

"Amen!" shouted Wood as the two made their way out the church, glowing in the noonday sun.

Made in the USA
Columbia, SC
31 May 2025